Beverly Lewis

Beverly Lewis Books for Young Readers

PICTURE BOOKS

In Jesse's Shoes • *Just Like Mama*
What Is God Like? • *What Is Heaven Like?*

THE CUL-DE-SAC KIDS

The Double Dabble Surprise
The Chicken Pox Panic
The Crazy Christmas Angel Mystery
No Grown-ups Allowed
Frog Power
The Mystery of Case D. Luc
The Stinky Sneakers Mystery
Pickle Pizza
Mailbox Mania
The Mudhole Mystery
Fiddlesticks
The Crabby Cat Caper
Tarantula Toes
Green Gravy
Backyard Bandit Mystery
Tree House Trouble
The Creepy Sleep-Over
The Great TV Turn-Off
Piggy Party
The Granny Game
Mystery Mutt
Big Bad Beans
The Upside-Down Day
The Midnight Mystery

Katie and Jake and the Haircut Mistake

www.BeverlyLewis.com

THE CUL-DE-SAC KIDS

The Chicken Pox Panic

Beverly Lewis

BETHANY HOUSE PUBLISHERS
MINNEAPOLIS, MINNESOTA 55438

© 1993 by Beverly Lewis

Originally published by Star Song Publishing Group under the same title. Bethany House Publishers edition published 1995.

Published by Bethany House Publishers
11400 Hampshire Avenue South
Bloomington, Minnesota 55438
www.bethanyhouse.com

Bethany House Publishers is a division of
Baker Publishing Group, Grand Rapids, Michigan

Printed in the United States of America by
Bethany Press International, Bloomington, MN
September 2014, 29th printing

ISBN 978-1-55661-626-6

The Library of Congress Cataloging-in-Publication Data
Lewis, Beverly.
  The chicken pox panic / Beverly Lewis.
    p. cm. —(The cul-de-sac kids ; 2)
    Summary: Chicken pox interfere with Abby's birthday surprise for her
• adopted Korean brother.
    ISBN 1-55661-626-0
    [1. Chicken pox—Fiction. 2. Brothers and sisters—Fiction. 3. Korean Americans—Fiction. 4. Birthdays—Fiction.] I. Title. II. Series : Lewis, Beverly. Cul-de-sac kids ; 2.
PZ7.L5846Ch 1994
[Fic]—dc20   94-49117

Interior illustrations by Barbarba Birch

14   15   16   17   18   19   20   35   34   33   32   31   30   29

To my very own
cul-de-sac kids

JULIE, JANIE,
and
JONATHAN

THE CUL-DE-SAC KIDS

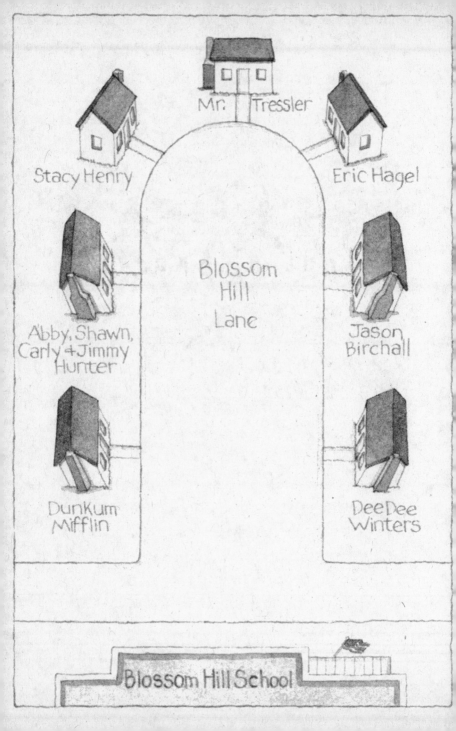

ONE

It was an itchy gitchy Friday.

Abby Hunter sat up in bed. She rubbed the spots on her arm. On her face. And behind her knees under her pajamas.

"I hate chicken pox," she said.

"Here," said her little sister, Carly. "Put this gooey stuff on."

She gave the bottle of pink liquid to Abby. Frowning at the spots, Carly backed away.

Abby shook the bottle and turned the lid. She wrinkled her nose. The spots on her nose wiggled. "Pee-uie. It stinks."

Slowly, one at a time, Abby dabbed pink goo on her spots.

It was supposed to make the itching stop.

Abby counted to ten, waiting for the pink goo to work. "Nothing's happening," she complained.

Carly leaned against the door. "I hope I don't get your chicken pox."

Abby dabbed another coating of goo on the bumps she could reach. "Mommy wants you to catch them," she said.

"How come?" Carly demanded.

"So you won't get them when you're grown-up."

Abby buttoned up her mint green bathrobe.

She felt cozy inside. Spots and all.

Carly stared at Abby, then she pointed. "Look, Abby! You even have them on your feet."

"I know," Abby said. "I have them everywhere!"

"What do they feel like?" Carly asked.

"Ever have a giant mosquito bite?"

Carly nodded.

"Just multiply that times one hundred," Abby said.

Carly shivered. She turned the door knob. "I'm getting out of here."

"You'll be sorry if you don't get them now," Abby said. She scratched between her toes.

"Will not," Carly said.

"Will so," Abby said.

"Will not," Carly said.

"Will . . ." Abby stopped.

Mother stood in the hallway carrying a large atlas. She gave it to Abby. "Is this what you need?"

Abby reached for the book of maps. "Thanks! This is double dabble good!"

She flipped the pages to the back of the atlas. "What's the capital of South Korea?"

"Seoul," said Mother, smoothing Abby's quilt.

Carly giggled. "That's a funny name."

Abby held the book open. "You just think it is. Come see how it's spelled."

"Not me," Carly said, hugging the door. "I'm staying right here."

Abby rolled her eyes. "Afraid of my chicken pox?"

Mother gave both girls a kiss. "It's not so bad having them when you are little," she said.

"That's what I told her," said Abby.

Mother grinned and left the room.

Abby turned to page 45 in the atlas.

She leaned on her elbows, looking at the map of South Korea. With her finger, she traced the borders.

"What are you doing?" Carly asked.

"It's a secret," said Abby.

Out of the corner of her eye, she saw Carly sneaking closer. Closer.

WHOOSH!

Abby plopped her pillow down on top of South Korea.

TWO

Abby climbed out of bed.

She went to her desk to find a ruler.

She kept her eyes on the pillow. The one hiding page 45 in the atlas.

It was time to measure South Korea. She sat on the edge of the bed. She held the pillow over the map, so Carly couldn't see.

Carly yelled, "You can't fool me. It's your homework!"

"Guess again," Abby said. She put the ruler down.

Carly stomped her foot. "Tell me this minute!"

Abby looked up from the map. "Don't be so bossy."

"Ple-e-ease, Abby?" Carly begged.

Abby looked into her sister's blue eyes. Could she trust her? "Do you promise not to tell?"

Carly grinned. "Cross my heart and hope to . . ."

"Don't say that," Abby said. "It's dumb."

"That's how you make a promise," Carly said.

"Maybe in first grade, but not in third." Abby picked up the pillow and uncovered the map.

Carly inched closer. "What's the map for?"

Abby scratched her nose. "Shawn used to live in Korea when his name was Li Sung Jin," she said.

"I know—before we adopted him and Jimmy."

Abby leaned on the atlas. "When Shawn and Jimmy came to live in America, they had to leave their country behind."

"I know that," said Carly. She played with her curls. "So what's the map for?"

"It's a double dabble surprise for Shawn's tenth birthday. He's going to have the best birthday cake ever!" Abby slammed the map book shut.

"I don't get it," Carly said. "Why are you looking at maps and talking about cakes?"

Abby smiled. "Just because."

She felt like a jitterbox inside. Birthday secrets did that. Always.

Carly tiptoed closer. Now she stood beside Abby's bed. "Please tell me." Carly crossed her heart.

"OK, OK. Here's my secret," said Abby. "I'm going to make a cake in the shape of South Korea for Shawn's party."

Carly jumped up and down. "Goody!"

"Remember, you can't tell anyone," said Abby. "The secret could get back to Shawn."

"And that would be terrible," said Carly. But she had a silly look on her face.

"You better not tell," Abby said. She slid under the covers.

"Or what?"

"Or you'll be sorry," Abby said. She pulled the quilt up. "I feel lousy."

"Chicken pox does that. Mommy said so." Carly opened the door to leave.

Abby was glad. She was tired of Carly's chatter. And all that dumb cross-your-heart stuff.

She hid the atlas under her bed.

Then she fell asleep wishing she hadn't told anyone about the cake.

THREE

Abby woke up when Carly brought in a supper tray. On it was chicken soup and honey toast.

Stacy Henry came for a visit. She was Abby's best friend.

Stacy pulled a get-well card out of her pocket.

"Here. I made this for you in art today." She gave it to Abby.

Abby read the card. It was a silly sad face with spots all over. It was Abby's itchy gitchy chicken pox face.

At the bottom of the card was a happy face—*after* the chicken pox.

11

"Hope you get well quick," Stacy said. She untied her sneakers and pulled them off.

"Thanks," Abby said. "I have to. My brother's birthday is in two weeks."

"And Abby's going to bake him a cake," Carly said.

Abby stared at Carly. *She better not tell!*

Carly put her hand over her mouth. "Oops, I mean, Abby's going to . . ."

"Just be quiet," Abby warned.

Abby wanted to take back the secret. Phooey, little sisters—what a pain!

Carly's friend, Dee Dee Winters, sneaked into the bedroom just then. She giggled when she saw Abby. "I brought you something, Abby-pox."

She gave Abby a plastic ring.

"Thanks," Abby said, sliding it on her pinky.

Carly stood beside the bed. "Wanna see Abby's spots?" She pulled back the covers.

Dee Dee's eyes got big.

"Come look," Abby said. She propped her

pillows up behind her, showing off the bumps.

"They're everywhere!" Dee Dee said.

Abby leaned against her pillows and grinned. "They kept me out of school all week."

Stacy sat on the edge of the bed.

"Look out or you'll catch them!" Carly shouted, pulling on Stacy's arm.

Stacy smiled. "It's OK. I had them last year."

Carly frowned. "You might get them again."

"Mother says you only get them once," Stacy said.

"Really?" said Carly.

Dee Dee crept toward the bed. "That's why I came over. My mother wants me to catch them." She held her breath like she was scared, but then she sat down on the bed.

"We could get them together," said Carly.

Dee Dee jumped up and said goodbye. She ran out of the room. Carly raced after her.

Abby slipped back under her quilt. "Quick, close the door," she said to Stacy.

Stacy hurried to shut the door. "Good idea. We have to talk."

"What's up?" asked Abby.

"Promise you won't tell?"

Abby sat straight up in bed. A secret!

"Well, *do* you?" Stacy unzipped the pocket on her jacket. She pulled out a piece of paper.

Abby nodded. "I promise."

She felt like a jitterbox for sure.

FOUR

Abby looked at Stacy's paper.

There was a tree with a bunch of branches and lines on it.

Stacy pointed to the paper. "Do you know what this is?"

Abby saw the names on the lines. "A family tree?"

Stacy nodded. "It's for school."

"Wish I could go back soon," said Abby. "Looks like fun."

"Not really," said Stacy.

"How come?"

"I asked my mother, and she didn't know very many names," said Stacy, sadly.

There were lots of blank lines in the branches on Stacy's paper.

Just then, someone knocked on the door.

"Shh!" said Stacy, sadly. She stuffed the paper into her pocket. "Don't say a word about this."

Abby nodded. Then she called, "Who is it?"

"Shawn," came the voice through the door. "Is Snow White in there?"

"Come look for your dog if you want," Abby said.

The door opened. In came Shawn waving a dog collar. "Snow White—gone."

"Are you sure?" Abby said.

"Carly say—time for Snow White to get chicken pox." Shawn looked worried.

Abby and Stacy giggled.

Shawn looked puzzled. "Dogs get pox?"

Abby smiled. "Definitely not."

"Good," said Shawn, smiling.

"Maybe Jimmy took Snow White for a

walk. Look for him, and you might find your dog," Abby suggested.

Shawn held up the dog collar. "Take dog walking without leash? Not smart."

"You're right," Abby said. She thought about Snow White's favorite place. "Look in the secret place, behind Carly's closet," she said. "Snow White likes to sleep there."

"Good thinking," Shawn said. He turned to Stacy. "Stay there. Do not leave soon." Then he ran out of the room.

Stacy looked surprised. "I wonder what he wants."

Abby said, "Quick! Show me your family tree again."

Stacy unfolded the paper. "Hurry, I don't want Shawn . . . uh, or anyone to see."

"Why not?" Abby asked.

"Because, I think I'm adopted." Stacy looked like she was going to cry.

"You do?" Abby said, surprised.

Stacy played with the zipper on her jacket.

"My mother can't find my baby pictures. Not a single one."

Abby scratched the bumps on her feet. "Maybe they got lost when you moved here."

"That was a long time ago," said Stacy.

"Wait a minute!" Abby said. "You can't be adopted. Everyone says your eyes look just like your dad's."

"That's what my mother says. But I don't remember him. He moved out years ago."

Abby took a deep breath. She wished Stacy's father lived at home. Right here on Blossom Hill Lane —the best cul-de-sac ever!

"I have an idea," said Abby. "Look at your birth certificate. It will tell you the truth."

"I tried that," Stacy said. "My mother can't find it either."

Abby frowned. "Is it lost?"

"I told you—I must be adopted," Stacy said. "Just like your Korean brothers and Snow White and . . ." She stopped.

Abby threw the covers off and scooted

19

across the bed. She put her arm around Stacy. "And what?"

"And if it's true, I don't even know where I came from."

Abby grabbed a Kleenex box off her dresser. "Here, wipe your eyes," she said. "Why don't you ask your mother?"

Stacy shook her head. "I did. She's too busy."

Now Abby was *really* worried.

Something was going on. She had to find out exactly what.

And fast!

FIVE

Someone pounded on Abby's bedroom door.

"Who's there?" Stacy called.

"Snow White and Goliath," said a tiny voice.

Abby giggled. "That must be Jimmy, my little brother."

Stacy tossed her family tree paper under the bed.

Jimmy came in carrying a fluffy white puppy. "Snow White sleeping in secret place . . . waiting for kiss from Goliath . . . to wake up," he said.

Abby and Stacy giggled.

"You have a fairy tale mixed in with a Bible story," Abby said. "Snow White is *not* in the Bible."

"And Goliath would never kiss a puppy," said Stacy.

"Jimmy's still learning about the Bible," Abby said. She liked telling her adopted brothers the story of David and Goliath. In Korea, they had only heard Bible stories in the orphanage. Nowhere else.

Jimmy grinned and put the puppy down. Snow White hopped up on the bed and licked Abby's face.

"No, no, Snow White," shouted Jimmy. "Must not get itchy pox."

Just then, Shawn came in with his school notebook.

Snow White leaped up on him, too.

"You are here!" said Shawn, petting his puppy. He put the collar on Snow White.

Then he showed his notebook to Stacy. He opened it to his family tree. He pointed to the grandfather line. "What did teacher say if person die?" he asked Stacy.

"You still write his name. Then the year he was born and the year he died. If you know it," Stacy said.

"Oh," Shawn said. "I do not know when grandfather die. Mother in Korea not know, too."

Abby scratched her neck. "Let's see your family tree," she said to Shawn.

There were two names on each line. One for his Korean birth parents and one for Abby's parents.

Shawn's eyes shone. "I have two families now."

Stacy peeked at Shawn's family tree. She pointed to the line on the left side. "Is this your birth mother's name?"

Shawn smiled. "Yes. First mother live in Korea. She very sick. Mrs. Hunter, Abby's mother, now my mother. She adopt Jimmy and me. We very lucky."

23

Stacy thought for a moment. "I think you're lucky, too."

Abby handed the notebook back. "Your writing is getting better, Shawn. I think it's an A + paper."

Shawn's eyes lit up. "Good. I think, too." Then he and Jimmy left the room.

Stacy sat on the rug, beside the bed. "I want to know if I'm adopted," she said.

"I'm good at solving mysteries," said Abby. "I'll help you."

"When can we start?" Stacy asked.

"As soon as my bumps crust over," said Abby.

Stacy leaned down and looked under the bed.

"What are you doing?" Abby said, remembering the atlas she hid there. She held her breath.

"Finding my family tree," said Stacy. "I hid it under here." She pulled out the book of maps. "Hey, what's this?"

Abby's heart beat fast. "A project I have."

She wished Stacy wouldn't ask.

"For school?" Stacy asked.

"Uh . . . no," said Abby, trying not to tell.

"What for?"

Abby scratched her head. "I can't tell." She pulled her knees up to her chin . . . thinking. About the doubly dabbly most creative birthday cake in the world!

"Come on, Abby. I can keep a secret," said Stacy.

"I know," Abby said.

"Then tell me, or I'll have to solve your mystery, too. I'll call it the Mystery of the Map Book," Stacy said.

Abby wasn't worried. Not one bit. Stacy couldn't solve a mystery even if she tried.

SIX

It was Wednesday.

Abby's bumps were scabby, so she went back to school.

At recess Stacy and Abby met near the swings.

"I have a plan," Abby said.

Stacy looked around to see if anyone was listening. "About my adoption?" she whispered.

Abby nodded. "When does your mother get home?"

"5:30."

"That gives us plenty of time. Today I'll solve your mystery," Abby said.

Stacy cheered, "All right! Meet me at my house after school."

When the bell rang after school, both girls raced toward Blossom Hill Lane—the cul-de-sac.

The wind was blowing hard.

Abby dug her hands into her coat pockets. A quarter was in one pocket. Three gummy bears were in the other.

Abby ran beside Stacy.

The cul-de-sac seemed quiet as they entered Stacy's house. Sunday Funnies, Stacy's cock-a-poo, barked as they came in the door. He shook his furry white head.

The girls headed straight for the master bedroom.

Stacy pointed to a file drawer. "My mother keeps important papers in there," she said.

Abby's heart pounded. She felt like a jitterbox inside. *This isn't right*, Abby worried. *We shouldn't be snooping.*

Then Abby looked at Stacy's face. This was

something important, and she wanted to help her friend.

Abby took a deep breath and pulled the handle.

Locked!

"Where's the key?" she asked.

"I don't know," said Stacy.

"Let's look around." Abby led the way.

First, to the closet. They looked in the shoe boxes. No key.

They looked in the lamp table beside the bed. A package of gum, some tissues, and a Bible were inside. But no key. Abby felt even worse about snooping.

"Where could it be?" asked Abby. "Think hard."

Stacy scratched her head. "Where would *you* hide a key?"

"Good question!" Abby dashed off to the kitchen.

"Now what?" asked Stacy.

Abby went to the refrigerator. She opened the freezer door. "This is the safest place in the house," Abby said. "In case of fire, the freezer is a good place to keep important stuff." She pulled three pizza boxes out.

Stacy took out a half gallon of ice cream. And bags of strawberries from her grandma's garden. There were frozen vegetables. A pot roast. Two bags of hot dogs. The girls stacked them on the floor.

Sunday Funnies sniffed at the carton of ice cream.

Abby peeked in the freezer. "Well, that's it. There's nothing left."

Then she spotted something shiny way in the back.

It was a key stuck to the side.

"Look at this!" shouted Abby, grabbing the key.

"You're amazing!" Stacy said as the girls raced back to the bedroom.

Abby turned the lock and opened the file drawer. "Look under the B's for birth certifi- cate," she said.

Stacy found the file folder and pulled it out.

Opening the folder, Abby saw only one birth certificate. It was Stacy's mother's.

"See what I mean?" said Stacy.

Abby thought for a minute. *Maybe Stacy is right. Maybe she is adopted!*

Detectives don't cry. But Abby sure felt like it when she saw Stacy's face. Being adopted was a *good* thing. Why hadn't Stacy's mother told her?

Then she remembered the freezer. And all the food. "Hurry, before your mom gets home!"

The girls raced to the kitchen.

"Oh, no!" cried Stacy. "I'm in trouble now."

Sunday Funnies crouched under the table. He had torn the pot roast open and was half finished with the ice cream. Chocolate ice cream was all over his face and paws.

"Quick! We have to do something before my mother gets home!"

Abby took the ice cream carton away from Sunday Funnies. She threw it in the trash with the slobbery pot roast.

The girls piled the rest of the food back into the freezer.

Then Stacy cleaned up the floor.

"I'll use my allowance to buy another roast. And some ice cream," Abby said. Then she remembered Shawn's birthday surprise.

Buying ice cream and a pot roast would use up all her savings.

Phooey! So much for the greatest cake in the world, she thought.

Abby hurried home to get her money. There was a huge lump in her throat.

SEVEN

It was starting to snow.

Abby hopped on her bike and headed for the grocery store. Snowflakes tickled her face.

She pedalled hard, thinking about the cake that could've been.

Now Shawn would never get his birthday cake. All because of the stupid detective stuff!

At the store, Abby found a roast. It looked like the one Sunday Funnies had torn open. She found the same brand of chocolate ice cream. She paid for it with every cent she had.

Pushing sad thoughts away, she headed for Stacy's. At last, she rang the doorbell.

"Come in!" called Stacy. "I'm in the bathroom giving my dog a bath. He's a chocolatey mess."

"I have another pot roast and some ice cream," Abby said. "Your mom will never have to know."

"Thanks," yelled Stacy. "Sorry about the money."

"It's my own dumb fault," Abby said. She went into the bathroom.

"No it isn't," Stacy said. She rubbed more soap on the puppy's head. "We were in it together."

"I've been thinking," Abby said. "It doesn't matter if you're adopted. Look how much your parents love you."

"I know that," said Stacy. "It's not so much being adopted . . . if I am. I just wish my parents had told me." Stacy sighed. "Your brothers, Shawn and Jimmy, know all about their adoption."

"They were older when it happened," Abby said. She heard the garage door open.

"Sounds like your mom's home," she said. "I better leave."

"No, wait," said Stacy. "I've got an idea."

"What?" Abby pulled a towel off the rack and handed it to Stacy.

"I'm going to ask my mother some questions. And I want you to listen." Stacy drained the dirty bath water.

There were footsteps in the hallway. "Stacy, I'm home," said her mother.

"Coming!" called Stacy. She lifted Sunday Funnies out of the tub.

Abby helped dry him.

"Follow me," Stacy said.

Abby followed her friend to the kitchen.

Stacy pulled a sheet of paper out of a drawer. She sat down at the table. Abby did, too.

Stacy took a deep breath. "I need to talk to you, Mom."

"Sure, honey. What's up?"

Stacy shot a nervous look at Abby. "What happened on the day I was born?"

"What do you mean, dear?" her mother asked.

"I need to know for my homework," Stacy said. "Were you there?"

Stacy's mother looked at her. She set the dishes on the counter. "Of course I was."

"How soon did you see me?" Stacy asked.

"A few hours after you were born."

Stacy laughed. "A few hours? That's a long time to wait, don't you think?"

Her mother opened a drawer and took out a spoon. "Why do you ask?"

Abby looked at Stacy. She held her breath.

Stacy stood up. "What happened to my birth certificate?"

"I really don't know," her mother said. "But we need to set the table now."

"Did you take any pictures of me when I was born?" Stacy asked.

Mrs. Henry pushed her hair back. She sighed. "I think your father did."

Stacy wrote something on her paper. "Does he still have them?"

"It's late now, Stacy. You know how sloppy I am at keeping records sometimes. Can we please talk about this later?" her mother said.

Abby stood up. "I better go home now. See you tomorrow, Stacy."

Stacy scrunched up her face. "OK, Abby."

Abby felt funny. Stacy's eyes didn't look like things were OK.

They spelled trouble. Big trouble!

Abby felt like a jitterbox.

Something was crazy wrong!

EIGHT

After supper Abby checked under her bed.

Good! The atlas was still there. Her sketch of South Korea marked the page. She stared at the map.

Then she looked at the teddy bear calendar on the wall. Only ten more days till Shawn's birthday!

Abby knelt beside her bed. She prayed, "Please, Lord, help me get some money for my brother's birthday party."

★ ★ ★

The next day Abby met Stacy in the lunch room. They sat at a long table next to the wall.

Abby leaned against the wall. "I have an idea, Stacy. Why don't you call your dad?"

"I've been thinking about it," Stacy said. She dipped a spoon into her chocolate pudding.

The girls next to them traded sticks of gum.

"You could ask your dad to send some of your baby pictures," Abby suggested.

"Great idea," Stacy said.

"Maybe he knows something about your birth certificate," Abby said, smiling. She hoped her idea would help.

"You're a good friend, Abby Hunter," Stacy said.

Abby felt warm inside.

"I'm going to call a meeting of the Cul-de-sac Kids," Stacy said.

"When? Why?"

"Tomorrow," said Stacy. "And don't ask so many questions." She had a sneaky smile.

"What's up?" Abby asked. Something was. She could see it in her friend's face!

"Wait and see," Stacy said. She went to dump her trash.

On Friday, everyone showed up at Dunkum's house. His real name was Edward Mifflin. He was a third grade hotshot on the basketball court.

Dunkum had the biggest basement in the cul-de-sac. That's where the kids liked to meet—in their socks. All the sneakers were lined up beside the stairs.

Abby sat in a bean bag near the TV. She was president. But today, Stacy was in charge.

The kids sat on the floor.

Stacy told them what her puppy had done. "Abby didn't want me to get in trouble. So she used up all her money to replace the roast and the ice cream. Now she needs a loan from us. For something very important."

Carly wiggled. Her eyes danced. Abby could tell she was having a hard time keeping the birthday secret.

Dunkum stood up. "Let's hear it for Abby. I'll loan her three bucks. Who will match it?"

Jason Birchall swayed back and forth. He could never sit still. Even with his hyper medicine. "I don't have three, but how's two-fifty?" he asked.

"We'll take it," said Dunkum. He smiled at Dee Dee Winters. "What about you? Got any cash to loan?"

"Just fifty cents." She pulled out two quarters. "The tooth fairy came last night." She showed the hole where her tooth had been.

Carly scooted over beside her.

Shawn raised his hand. "I save money. I give money to Abby." He stood up and emptied his pockets.

Shawn handed the money to Dunkum.

Abby didn't want her brother's money. It was going for *his* cake! "Uh, that's plenty without Shawn's," she said, quickly.

Eric Hagel whistled. "Hey, what about me? I have a dollar," he said. "And Abby doesn't ever have to pay me back."

"Thanks," Dunkum said, reaching for it.

Abby wished they would stop. God had answered her prayer with more than enough money for Shawn's cake.

She waved her hands. "Yo, kids!"

"The president of the Cul-de-sac Kids wants to speak," Stacy announced.

The kids got quiet. Even Carly and Dee Dee.

"Thanks for helping me out," Abby said. "I'll pay each of you back as soon as I can. Now, I want to invite everyone to a birthday party for my brother next Saturday. Come over after lunch."

Shawn's eyebrows shot up, then he grinned.

The kids cheered. "All right Shawn! Hurray for Abby!"

The meeting was over. The sneaker scramble began.

Dee Dee got Carly's by mistake. They were red, too, but bigger.

After the kids left, Stacy sat beside Abby. "I'm going to call my father tonight," Stacy said.

Abby stretched her legs. "That's double dabble good!"

Stacy smiled. "I think it's time to ask him a few questions."

The girls got up and found their sneakers.

Abby's were mismatched. One red, one blue.

"Be sure and tell me what he says," Abby said. She put the money in her jeans pocket. "Thanks for helping. You're a good friend, Stacy Henry."

Abby ran all the way home. She had a birthday party to plan. Things were definitely terrific.

Nothing could go wrong now!

NINE

The next morning, Abby dashed over to Stacy's. "Did you call your dad?"

Stacy stood in the doorway. She zipped up her jacket. "I chickened out."

"Oh," said Abby. She wished Stacy wasn't so nervous about it.

They rode their bikes to the store. It was time to buy the birthday stuff.

Abby couldn't make up her mind. Should she buy blue balloons? Or red ones?

"This is my Korean brother's first birthday in America," said Abby.

"Get him American colors," Stacy suggested.

So Abby bought red, white, and blue balloons.

Later, they hid the party stuff under Abby's bed. Then Stacy went home.

★ ★ ★

After lunch, Stacy phoned. "Can I come over?" She sounded excited.

"Sure," Abby said, pulling off her sneakers.

Ding dong! The doorbell rang.

Abby ran to the front door in her socks.

Stacy flew in the door, grabbing Abby's arm. "I'm NOT adopted!"

"How do you know?"

"I called my dad. He has my birth certificate. And he's going to send me a copy!"

They dashed upstairs to Abby's bedroom.

"And that's not all," Stacy said. "He wants to come visit me sometime."

Abby closed the door. This was super double dabble good!

Stacy sat on the rug. So did Abby.

"This is the best day of my life," Stacy said. She pulled off her sneakers. "The mystery of my birth is solved."

Abby laughed. "And *you* solved it!" She reached under the bed and pulled out a bag of balloons.

"If you need any help with the party, let me know," Stacy said. "I'm not the best detective, but I'm a good fixer-upper."

Abby ripped open the balloon bag. "Can you blow up balloons?"

"Sure," said Stacy. And she blew up a blue one. It made her face bright red.

Abby clapped for her. "I can't wait for the party."

Just then, Carly came into the room. She had pink bumps on her arms and face. She was moaning.

"Look who's got chicken pox," Stacy said.

"Oh, no," Abby gasped. "Stay away from Shawn."

"That's right!" Stacy snapped. "If he gets them, there goes the party!"

Abby jumped up and led Carly off to her own room.

TEN

It was three days before Shawn's party.

Little Jimmy was sick in bed with chicken pox. Itchy spots were in his nose and in his hair. They were nearly everywhere!

Dee Dee Winters had them, too. And Jason Birchall missed school.

Abby was worried. *Who's next?*

Two days before the party, Eric and Dunkum broke out with chicken pox. After supper Shawn did, too.

"Rats!" Abby said to her mother. "Now we can't have the party."

"But you can still bake a cake," her mother said. "Shawn would like that."

The next day, Abby hurried to the kitchen. She got out mixing bowls, eggs, and flour. Baking powder, sugar, chocolate squares, and canned frosting.

She posted the pattern of South Korea on the refrigerator with a clown magnet. Next she tiptoed to the boys' room. They were sound asleep. Good!

Back in the kitchen, she followed her mother's recipe. When she measured the flour and the sugar, some of it flew onto the floor. When she mixed the batter, it spilled, too. What a mess!

At last, she slid the cake pans into the oven and waited.

When the timer rang, Abby used the hot pads. The oven was very hot—so were the cake pans. She placed them on the counter to cool.

Then Abby heard footsteps. She turned around. There was Jimmy, making flour footprints on the floor. Snow White was behind him, licking up spilled sugar.

Abby stared at her little brother. "What are you doing up?"

"Thirsty," Jimmy moaned.

Abby poured a glass of water. "Here," she said, holding the glass out to him. "Now go back to bed."

"Not tired," he said, scratching his spots.

"Don't scratch," Abby said. "It'll make marks."

He walked to the refrigerator tracking flour everywhere. Reaching for the map of South Korea, Jimmy slipped and fell.

"Ouch!" he cried.

Abby helped him back to bed. Shawn was still asleep.

Whew! Close call.

Gotta hurry, thought Abby tiptoeing back to the kitchen.

She turned the first cake pan upside down. It was so hot it burned her fingers. The cake came out in a crumbly mess on the plate.

Oh, no! What's wrong? she thought.

Then she remembered Stacy—the fixer-

upper. Abby called her best friend on the phone. She came right over.

"I want it to look like South Korea," Abby said pointing to the map. "Shawn's birthday is tomorrow!"

Stacy grabbed the drawing off the fridge. "So *this* is the secret you were keeping from me."

"Please help me, Stacy," Abby whispered. "I'll never keep secrets from you again, I promise."

Stacy smiled. "It's a deal. Now, first of all, the pans have to cool before you dump out the cake," she explained. "But I think I can fix your mess."

Abby watched as Stacy worked.

Bit by bit, she pieced the cake together with canned frosting. But the cake had ugly bumps and ridges in it.

It looked more like the Grand Canyon than South Korea!

Soon, the second cake pan was cool

enough. Stacy turned it over, but the cake was stuck!

Stacy groaned. "Why didn't you butter and flour the pan first?"

"I thought I did."

Stacy tried one more time to get the cake out of the pan. But it fell out in pieces.

Abby looked at the cake in horror. "Oh, no!" she cried.

"Oh, forget it. Just get me a streamer," Stacy said.

"What for?"

"To hold the cake together," Stacy said.

Abby had never heard of such a thing. Did Stacy really know what she was doing?

Abby ran to her room to get the red streamers. There was no time to waste.

ELEVEN

Abby rushed back to the kitchen with red streamers and tape.

Stacy wrapped the streamer around the cake. She stuck tape on the end. Then she stepped back to have a look.

Abby felt like a jitterbox. She didn't know what to think of Stacy's repair job. "Shouldn't we frost it all over?" Abby asked.

"When it cools some more." Stacy slid the two layer cake into the freezer. When she closed the door she leaned against it. "Remember that pot roast you bought with your own money?"

Abby felt jittery. "Sure, why?"

"Well, my mother noticed it was a different brand. So I told her what we did." Stacy paused. "I told her everything."

"I'm glad you did," Abby said. "I knew we were wrong."

Stacy grinned and washed her hands. "She wants you to come for supper tonight."

"She does?"

Stacy laughed. "We're having your pot roast."

Abby's jitters were gone. "I'll tell your mother I'm sorry in person," she said.

Then she set the timer. In fifteen minutes she would check the cake.

When Stacy left, Abby sat at the kitchen table. She thought about Shawn's chicken pox. She thought about the birthday cake. What an icky mess it was—even with the red streamer holding it together. The white frosting could never hide the ugly mess. It still looked like the Grand Canyon. Instead of South Korea.

Then Abby had an idea. She searched in

the pantry and found what she needed. A bag of red cherry chips.

Abby's cake still had a chance. It would be first-rate after all. Her cake could have the chicken pox!

The red cherry chips would hide the lumpy bumpy cake. It was perfect.

Abby danced a jig around the kitchen.

The buzzer rang.

Abby jigged to the freezer and took out the cake.

Ready!

★　★　★

The next day was Shawn's birthday. Abby got up early and decorated the kitchen with red, white, and blue balloons. Even though the party was off, she wanted to surprise Shawn.

After lunch, the doorbell rang. When Abby opened the door, there stood the Cul-de-sac Kids. Chicken pox and all!

"Surprise!" they shouted. "Surprise on you, Abby Hunter!"

Letting her friends inside, Abby giggled. It was definitely a good surprise.

The kids cheered when they saw the kitchen.

Abby gave everyone a red marker. "Let's put red spots everywhere. We'll give every-thing the chicken pox!" she said.

And that's what they did.

The balloons and the napkins were spotted. Even the streamers had pox dots!

Abby put red sticker dots on the dog. Now Snow White had chicken pox, too. She barked and ran around in circles.

Abby's mother invited everyone to sit down. Then Shawn peeked around the corner in his pajamas. He grinned at his spotty friends.

"Surprise!" they shouted. "Happy Birthday!"

Abby pulled out a chair for her brother. It was at the head of the table. Then she carried in the lumpy, bumpy cake with white frosting. And red cherry chip chicken pox spots.

Mother lit the birthday candles. They were white with red polka dots. "Happy, happy birthday, son," she said.

"Make a wish," Abby said.

Shawn closed his eyes. There were spots on his eyelids.

Then Shawn blew out ten candles on the first try.

Everyone cheered. Abby wanted to dance.

It was a super itchy gitchy Saturday, so the party was short. But it didn't matter.

The Cul-de-sac Kids said it was the best pox party ever!

THE CRAZY CHRISTMAS ANGEL MYSTERY

What's going on at Mr. Tressler's house? Why is the living room always flickering with candlelight? What about the spooky flute music before dawn? Eric Hagel plans to find out. When the old man puts up a Christmas tree, the angel at the top comes to life! Soon, dozens of angels are flying around in the old man's house.

Can Eric and the Cul-de-sac Kids solve the mystery? And who will be brave enough to take a gift to the house at the end of Blossom Hill Lane?

ABOUT THE AUTHOR

Beverly Lewis remembers waiting for the mail as a kid. She wrote lots of letters to pen pals and other friends. (Still does!)

Beverly and her younger sister, Barbara, had lots of fun with their neighborhood friends. They made "Mushy Goo-Goo"—a secret recipe that included a little water and lots of dirt. They dressed their cats in doll clothes. They hitched up Maxie, their Eskimo Spitz, to a sled and went to the store in a blizzard.

They even had a carnival to raise money for a Jerry's Kids Telethon. And ended up in the newspaper, and later got to be on TV!

If you like books that tickle your funny bone, look for Beverly's next books in the Cul-de-sac Kids series.

Visit Beverly's Web site at *www.BeverlyLewis.com*.

Also by Beverly Lewis

Adult Nonfiction
Amish Prayers
The Beverly Lewis Amish Heritage Cookbook

Adult Fiction

HOME TO HICKORY HOLLOW
The Fiddler • The Bridesmaid • The Guardian
The Secret Keeper • The Last Bride

SEASONS OF GRACE
The Secret • The Missing • The Telling

ABRAM'S DAUGHTERS
The Covenant • The Betrayal • The Sacrifice • The Prodigal
The Revelation

ANNIE'S PEOPLE
The Preacher's Daughter • The Englisher • The Brethren

THE ROSE TRILOGY
The Thorn • The Judgment • The Mercy

THE COURTSHIP OF NELLIE FISHER
The Parting • The Forbidden • The Longing

THE HERITAGE OF LANCASTER COUNTY
The Shunning • The Confession • The Reckoning

OTHER ADULT FICTION
The Postcard • The Crossroad • The Redemption of Sarah Cain
October Song • Sanctuary* • The Sunroom • Child of Mine*

Youth Fiction

Girls Only (GO!) Volume One and *Volume Two[†]*
SummerHill Secrets Volume One and *Volume Two[†]*
Holly's Heart Collection One[‡], Collection Two[‡],
and Collection Three[†]

www.BeverlyLewis.com·

[*]with David Lewis   [†]4 books in each volume   [‡]5 books in each volume

From Bethany House Publishers

Fiction for Young Readers

(ages 7–10)

AstroKids™
by Robert Elmer

Space scooters? Floating robots? Jupiter ice cream? Blast into the future for out-of-this-world, zero-gravity fun with the AstroKids on space station *CLEO-7*.

The Cul-de-sac Kids
by Beverly Lewis

Each story in this lighthearted series features the hilarious antics and predicaments of nine endearing boys and girls who live on Blossom Hill Lane.

Janette Oke's Animal Friends
by Janette Oke

Endearing creatures from the farm, forest, and zoo discover their place in God's world through various struggles, mishaps, and adventures.